YOGA ANIMALS
AT THE SEASHORE

CHRISTIANE KERR & JASON HOOK

ILLUSTRATED BY JULIA GREEN

Kane Miller
A DIVISION OF EDC PUBLISHING

ABOUT THIS BOOK

In this book, you will read about Crab's day at the seashore.

Along the way, Crab will meet friends who will teach him how to do some simple yoga poses.

First, Crab will learn why each pose is helpful, and you'll see him try them out.

Then, it's your turn.

Look at the panel at the bottom of each page, like the example below. Don't worry if you don't get it right the first time— keep practicing and have fun!

Read the instructions to follow the pose.

The pictures will show you each step.

CAN YOU DO IT, TOO?

1. Lie on your back with your feet flat on the floor and your knees pointing up toward the sky, arms by your sides with palms facing up.

2. As you breathe in, slowly reach your legs and arms up. As you breathe out, keep your back on the ground and let your arms and legs gently move around, like seaweed floating in the water.

The yoga exercises in this book should be practiced with the help of an adult. It is recommended that children attempt the poses on a yoga mat. For the full benefits of each pose, see pages 30—31.

Crab woke up at the bottom
of his tide pool, feeling
a little cold and stiff.

"When I wake
up," said Pipefish,
"I stretch and
S-T-R-E-T-C-H
like this."

4

Crab stretched,
just like Pipefish.
And Crab began
to feel warmer.

CAN YOU DO IT, TOO?

1. Sit with your back straight and your legs crossed. Hold your ankles with your hands.

2. Breathe in as you round your back. Bring your shoulders and head forward and drop your chin to your chest.

3. As you breathe out, pull your chest forward and look up at the sky.

4. Repeat three times.

Crab was still feeling grumpy. He really didn't want to leave his tide pool.

"When I feel grumpy," said Seal, "I float on my back like this."

6

Crab felt himself float,
just like Seal. And as
he looked up to the sky,
Crab started to smile.

CAN YOU DO IT, TOO?

1. Lie on your back with your feet flat on the floor and your knees pointing up toward the sky, arms by your sides with palms facing up.

2. As you breathe in, slowly reach your legs and arms up. As you breathe out, keep your back on the ground and let your arms and legs gently move around, like seaweed floating in the water.

Crab's head was full of thoughts— should he go in the ocean, or not?

"When I don't know what to do," said Sea Otter, "I stand still like this."

Crab stood still, just like Sea Otter.
And Crab decided he would go in the ocean.

CAN YOU DO IT, TOO?

 1. Stand up straight with your feet slightly apart, arms by your sides.

 2. Breathe in as you raise your arms above your head, keeping them in line with your ears. As you breathe out, bend your knees and imagine you are pressing your feet into soft, warm sand.

3. Stay here for three breaths, repeating quietly, "Every breath helps me focus."

Crab looked at the water and tried not to be nervous—the waves seemed very powerful.

"I lift one leg and balance when I want to feel strong," said Seagull.

Crab lifted a leg and balanced, just like Seagull.

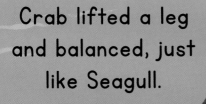

And Crab felt like he could do anything.

CAN YOU DO IT, TOO?

1. Stand up straight with your feet hip-distance apart.

2. Breathe in and raise your left arm above your head. As you breathe out, lift and bend your right knee back so you can hold your foot with your right hand.

3. Look straight ahead and take three quiet breaths as you balance. (If you feel wobbly, you can practice this pose by placing your raised hand against a wall.) Repeat on the other side.

Crab walked into the ocean. As the water got deeper, he started to feel very alone.

"When I feel alone," said Starfish, "I spread my arms out as wide as I can."

Crab spread out,
just like Starfish.
And Crab felt OK
being by himself.

CAN YOU DO IT, TOO?

 1. Stand with your feet slightly apart, arms by your sides.

 2. Take a big breath in and as you breathe out, jump your feet wide and stretch your arms out above your head.

3. Wiggle your fingers as you take three breaths, repeating quietly, "The ground beneath my feet helps me reach the sky."

Crab explored the ocean
floor. But he felt unsure.
Was here in the ocean
the best place to be?

"When I feel unsure,"
said Hermit Crab,
"I point like this."

14

Crab pointed, just like Hermit Crab. And Crab knew he'd made the right decision.

CAN YOU DO IT, TOO?

1. Stand with your feet slightly apart, arms by your sides.

2. Take a big step back with your left foot, turning your toes to face outward. Lift your arms in line with your shoulders, right arm forward and left arm back, keeping a straight line between your hands. Bend your right knee.

3. Breathe in and, as you breathe out, say quietly, "I am strong and ready to face anything that comes my way." Repeat on the other side.

Crab explored among the rocks, but it was hard to climb over them, and he felt frustrated.

"I do this when I want to calm my mind," said Butterfly Ray.

16

Crab reached up,
just like Butterfly Ray.
And Crab felt calmer.

CAN YOU DO IT, TOO?

1. Stand with your feet slightly apart, arms by your sides.

2. Breathe in and slowly reach your arms above your head. Stand up onto your tiptoes.

3. As you breathe out, lower your arms and feet back down. Repeat quietly, "I am calm and steady."

Crab had been so busy
that he felt quite tired.
But there was so much
more he wanted to see.

"I do this when
I need energy,"
said Dolphin.

Crab made himself long, just like Dolphin. And Crab felt energized.

CAN YOU DO IT, TOO?

1. Kneel down on all fours, keeping your arms straight and the palms of your hands on the ground.

2. Curl your toes under and slowly straighten your legs as you raise your bottom into the air. Press your arms and legs into the ground. Imagine you are light and free, like a dolphin surfing the waves.

Crab could see some
fish playing. They looked
like they were having
fun! But he was too
shy to join in.

"When I feel shy,"
said Eel, "I do this."

Crab lay back, just like Eel.
And Crab felt braver—now
he wanted to play, too!

CAN YOU DO IT, TOO?

1. Lie on your back with your knees bent, feet flat on the floor, and arms by your sides.

2. As you breathe in, press your feet into the ground and lift your hips. As you breathe out, stretch your arms up over your head and rest them on the ground behind you.

3. Repeat three times.

Crab played hide-and-seek in the seaweed. He felt so happy with his new friends.

"When I'm happy, I puff out like this," said Clownfish.

Crab puffed out, just
like Clownfish. And Crab
felt even happier!

CAN YOU DO IT, TOO?

1. Lie on your tummy, with your legs straight out behind you. Rest your forehead on your hands.

2. Keep your right leg straight and stretch your right arm out in front of you. Bend your left knee and hold your foot with your left hand, lifting your head. Take three breaths here, then rest. Repeat on the other side.

3. Hold both of your feet, pressing them into your hands as you feel your chest opening and lifting. Take three breaths here.

By the time Crab got back to the beach, it was getting dark. He started to worry about finding his way home.

"When I get worried," said Pelican, "I settle down like this."

Crab settled down, just like Pelican.
And when Crab closed his eyes,
his worries seemed to float away.

CAN YOU DO IT, TOO?

1. Sit with your legs bent in front of you, hip-distance apart, feet flat on the ground.

2. Put your arms between your legs and your hands on the ground, and lean forward. Hold the outside of your ankles, bringing the soles of your feet together.

3. You can stay in pose 2, or if it feels comfy, lean farther forward and rest your head on your feet. Breathe quietly as you relax here.

Back in his tide pool, Crab was so excited from the day he'd had that he thought he would never get to sleep.

"After I've had an exciting day," said Sea Snail, "I sit and think like this."

Crab sat and thought,
just like Sea Snail.

And Crab remembered
all the creatures who had
shared their day with him.

CAN YOU DO IT, TOO?

1. Kneel down with your bottom resting on your heels and your back straight.

2. Fold your body over your legs and rest your forehead on the ground with your arms stretched forward. Bend your elbows and rest the palms of your hands on your shoulders. Feel your body move as you take three big breaths in and out.

3. As you lie here, being very quiet and still, think about all the things you did today.

Crab had learned to stretch like Pipefish, float like Seal, stand still like Sea Otter, balance like Seagull, spread out like Starfish, point like Hermit Crab, reach up like Butterfly Ray, be long like Dolphin, lie back like Eel, puff out like Clownfish, settle down like Pelican, and sit and think like Sea Snail. But now all he wanted to do was ...

... sleep like Crab.

CAN YOU DO IT, TOO?

1. Lie on your tummy and bring your hands in front of you, one on top of the other. Place your forehead on your hands and let your body relax. Breathe in and feel where your body touches the ground. As you breathe out, let your body become soft.

2. Repeat quietly, "My body and mind are quiet and relaxed."

POSE BENEFITS

STRETCH LIKE PIPEFISH

- Stretches the front and back of the torso
- Increases flexibility of the spine
- Promotes calm
- Develops breath awareness

FLOAT LIKE SEAL

- Grounding
- Promotes calm
- Relaxes and lengthens the spine
- Stretches the hips and shoulders

STAND STILL LIKE SEA OTTER

- Strengthens the legs
- Stretches the shoulders and chest
- Increases focus and concentration

BALANCE LIKE SEAGULL

- Opens the chest
- Improves posture
- Strengthens the legs
- Builds confidence

SPREAD OUT LIKE STARFISH

- Grounding
- Improves posture
- Stretches the spine
- Opens the chest

POINT LIKE HERMIT CRAB

- Builds confidence
- Strengthens the whole body
- Increases focus and concentration

REACH UP LIKE BUTTERFLY RAY

- Develops breath and body awareness
- Promotes calm
- Builds confidence

BE LONG LIKE DOLPHIN

- Energizing
- Strengthens the whole body
- Stretches the legs and spine

LIE BACK LIKE EEL

- Promotes calm
- Helps with sleep issues
- Stretches the chest, neck, and spine
- Builds confidence

PUFF OUT LIKE CLOWNFISH

- Opens the chest
- Increases flexibility of the spine
- Improves digestion

SETTLE DOWN LIKE PELICAN

- Stretches the back, hips, and legs
- Promotes calm

SIT AND THINK LIKE SEA SNAIL

- Develops breath awareness
- Promotes calm
- Builds happiness

SLEEP LIKE CRAB

- Promotes calm
- Relaxing
- Develops breath and body awareness

31

First American Edition 2021
Kane Miller, A Division of EDC Publishing

Copyright © 2021 Quarto Publishing plc

For information contact:
Kane Miller, A Division of EDC Publishing
PO Box 470663
Tulsa, OK 74147-0663
www.kanemiller.com
www.edcpub.com
www.usbornebooksandmore.com

Library of Congress Control Number: 2020936360

Manufactured in Guangdong, China TT112020

ISBN: 978-1-68464-169-7

2 3 4 5 6 7 8 9 10